ADAM SHARP
· Operation Spy School ·

by George Edward Stanley
illustrated by Guy Francis

A STEPPING STONE BOOK™

Random House 🏠 New York

To Gwen, James, and Charles—
how can I be so lucky?
—G.E.S.

For Koltan and Wyatt
—G.F.

Text copyright © 2003 by George Edward Stanley. Illustrations copyright © 2003
by Guy Francis. All rights reserved under International and Pan-American Copyright
Conventions. Published in the United States by Random House Children's Books,
a division of Random House, Inc., New York, and simultaneously in Canada by
Random House of Canada Limited, Toronto.

www.randomhouse.com/kids

Library of Congress Cataloging-in-Publication Data
Stanley, George Edward.
Adam Sharp, Operation Spy School / by George Edward Stanley ;
illustrated by Guy Francis.
    p.   cm. — (A stepping stone book)
SUMMARY: Adam Sharp and others of IM-8 go back to spy school to learn
the newest tricks, but an enemy spy has infiltrated the top-secret classes.
ISBN 0-375-82404-9 (pbk.) — ISBN 0-375-92404-3 (lib. bdg.)
[1. Spies—Fiction.] I. Francis, Guy, ill. II. Title. III. Series.
PZ7.S78694Ae 2003 [Fic]—dc21 2002154479

Printed in the United States of America First Edition 10 9 8 7 6 5 4 3 2 1

Contents

1

The Spies Have Landed!

A big orange school bus raced toward the Friendly Airport. Inside, IM-8 agent Adam Sharp held on tight.

T was driving. T was the head of IM-8, a top-secret international spy agency. Adam was its best agent.

T and Adam were on their way to pick up IM-8 agents from all over the world.

Today was the first day of Operation Spy School. Its purpose was to teach all the agents the latest spy tricks.

Up ahead, Adam saw the lights of the airport. A huge plane had just landed.

T pulled the bus up beside it.

Tulip Belle, Magna Carter, and Kay Largo came off the plane first. Adam knew them from secret IM-8 missions.

"*Goedendag,* Tulip," Adam said. "Hullo, Magna. What's up, Kay?"

"Blimey, Adam," Magna said. "Spy School is a great idea!"

"Of course," Adam said. "Even the best spies can always get better!"

"Dude!" Kay said. "When Spy School is over, no evil person will be safe!"

Everyone boarded the bus, and T drove to Friendly Elementary School. A big banner stretched across the school's door. It said WELCOME TO THE GIFTED AND TALENTED JAMBOREE.

There wasn't really a Gifted and Talented Jamboree here this weekend. It was just a cover for Operation Spy School.

T took everyone on a tour. When it was over, he took them to the gym. It had been turned into a dormitory. While Adam helped Tulip, Magna, and Kay unpack, they talked about the missions they had gone on.

Suddenly, a voice over the loudspeaker boomed, "All Gifted and Talented students report to the cafeteria immediately!"

Adam tensed. Was something wrong?

The voice went on, "It's time to eat!"

"Blimey! We have to eat in a cafeteria?" Magna said. "I fancied some *good* food!"

"The food is great here," Adam said.

"*Ja,* you're lucky," Tulip said. "Most cafeteria food is gross."

"Not when Mrs. Sweet is the cook," Adam said. "She's the best!"

Mrs. Sweet had come to Friendly Elementary School three months before. Now kids begged their parents to let them eat the school lunches. No one wanted to bring their own anymore. Even the teachers lined up for Mrs. Sweet's lunches.

Mrs. Sweet worked very hard, and she was a nice person, too. Between classes, she baked chocolate chip cookies for the Friendly Nursing Home.

Every day the nursing home sent a big black car to the front of the school. Mrs. Sweet ran out and handed the driver a box filled with her famous cookies.

Adam had asked T if Mrs. Sweet could cook for Spy School.

"It will be all right," Adam had told T. "Mrs. Sweet will think she's cooking for the Gifted and Talented Jamboree."

T had said, "Okay."

Mrs. Sweet had even offered to sleep in the cafeteria—just in case someone needed a midnight snack. That's how nice she was!

When they got to the cafeteria, Adam introduced Tulip, Magna, and Kay to Mrs.

Sweet. Mrs. Sweet put an extra chocolate chip cookie on each of their trays.

"Yum!" Kay said. "My favorite!"

They took their trays to a table.

"Mrs. Sweet is so neat," Magna said. She was turning her cookies around and around. "Hey! Some of these chocolate chips are in strange patterns!"

Everyone laughed.

"Oh, Magna, they're just cookies," Tulip said. "You're always thinking like a spy."

Magna ducked her head and blushed. She took her job very seriously. They all did.

When they had finished eating, they went to the auditorium for an expert judo class. Afterward, it was time for lights out.

"We have to be up early for the IM-8 Obstacle Course Test," Adam reminded them.

Everyone shivered. If you couldn't pass that test, you couldn't be an IM-8 agent!

2

Stranger, Danger!

Adam was awake before dawn. T had asked him to make sure the obstacle course was ready. Actually, all Adam had to do was put up a few signs.

That's because the school's playground was already an IM-8 obstacle course!

It had tunnel slides to teach you how to crawl through narrow caves. It had monkey bars to teach you how to swing on vines through jungles. It had car tires to teach you how to jump from rock to rock on the side of a mountain.

In fact, from time to time, other government agencies trained there after dark. Adam had seen the FBI, the Marines, and even the Navy Seals.

Adam gave the obstacle course a final check. *Perfect,* he thought.

The bell rang. The IM-8 agents came running out the door. They lined up in formation. T followed them outside.

"IM-8 agents must be fit," T said. "If you can pass the IM-8 Obstacle Course

Test, you can beat any evil person in the world!"

Everyone cheered.

Just as T started giving directions, Adam saw a man hiding behind the hedge at the edge of the playground. No one was supposed to be there!

The man had on a black trench coat, a black hat, and sunglasses. He was definitely watching them.

"I'm going in, Tulip!" Adam whispered.

Adam ran to the side of the school. He got down on his hands and knees and crawled through the hedge. He stood up slowly.

The stranger was writing in a little notebook. He was not just a stranger! He was a spy!

Adam raced across the blacktop. The spy saw Adam coming. He jumped through the hedge and headed for the playground.

Big mistake! Adam thought. Now the spy had to pass the IM-8 Obstacle Course Test to escape. There was no way *that* would happen!

But the spy swung on the monkey bars with ease.

Adam swung on the monkey bars.

The spy crawled through the tunnel slide. No problem.

Adam crawled through the tunnel slide.

The spy jumped through the tires without even looking at his feet.

Adam jumped through the tires. He had to peek at his feet twice.

He's really good! Adam thought. *But wait until he hits the mud pit!* The mud pit was known for sucking off sneakers and swallowing playground balls.

But the spy did a perfect ninja roll in the mud.

Adam started a perfect ninja roll. He was only halfway through it when the spy whipped off his trench coat and threw it at Adam. The coat covered Adam's head. He fell into the mud.

He couldn't see! But he could smell
something. Chocolate chip cookies!

In the seconds it took Adam to get the
trench coat off, the spy got away.

Tulip, Magna, and Kay ran up to
Adam. "Blimey, Adam!" Magna said. "Who
was that?"

"A spy!" Adam said.

The girls gasped.

"Hurry," Adam told them. "We have to look for clues while the trail is hot!" He got down on his knees and searched the ground.

He picked up some brown crumbs. "That thief!" Adam clenched his fists. "He was stealing Mrs. Sweet's cookies!"

"Dude! That is *so* evil!" Kay said. "How did he know IM-8 was here?"

"Someone must be leaking IM-8 secrets," Adam said.

Adam, Tulip, Magna, and Kay stared at each other. *There was a spy in Spy School!*

3
Big-Time
Security Breakdown

Adam opened his eyes. It was morning, and Mrs. Sweet was standing by his cot.

"Here's your breakfast, dearie," Mrs. Sweet whispered.

Adam yawned. He had stayed up late trying to figure out who the spy was. He thought it might be a new IM-8 agent working for the other side.

Mrs. Sweet put the tray down next to him. A blueberry muffin, an omelet, orange juice, and milk.

"Wow!" Adam said softly.

Mrs. Sweet sat on the cot. "You're so gifted and talented, Adam," she said. "I wish I were smart like you!"

"You're smart, too, Mrs. Sweet," Adam said. "You know how to cook everything."

"That's not enough," Mrs. Sweet said sadly. She sighed. Then she stood up and quietly left the gym.

Adam felt sorry for Mrs. Sweet. Maybe cooking wasn't all that fulfilling for her.

He thought for a minute. *I'll talk to T,* he decided. *There may be a place for Mrs. Sweet in IM-8!*

Adam dressed quickly. It was time for J's gadget class. J was the janitor at Friendly Elementary School, but he also worked for IM-8. He made all the gadgets that IM-8 agents used for spying.

As the IM-8 agents filed into the classroom, Adam studied them carefully.

Which one is giving away IM-8 secrets? he asked himself.

"Good morning, class!" J said.

"Good morning, sir!" the class said.

"As you know, it is important for spies to blend in with their surroundings," J began. Adam nodded and straightened his bow tie. "So I have developed a line of spy gadgets using regular school supplies."

J picked up an eraser. He erased some writing on the chalkboard. Suddenly, he threw the eraser at a dummy in a corner of the room. The eraser exploded into a huge ball of chalk dust.

"That dummy spy can't see a thing

now!" J announced between coughs.

"Neither can we!" someone called.

J ignored him and went on. He showed the class a brown bottle. "Glue!" he said.

He squirted some onto the desk. He rolled it into a long, sticky rope and tied up Magna.

She couldn't get free. Even the whirling saw blades in the heels of her boots wouldn't cut the sticky rope!

J had to use a special blowtorch.

"Now I'm going to show you a power pencil," J said. "It has two tiny rockets—"

Just then, the classroom door opened.

J stopped talking.

Who could that be? Adam wondered. No one was allowed in the classroom except IM-8 agents.

A head appeared. It was Mrs. Sweet!

"Yoo-hoo, Adam!" she called. She motioned for him to come to the door.

Adam looked at J.

J shrugged.

Adam went to the door. "What's wrong, Mrs. Sweet?" he whispered.

"Nothing. I baked chocolate chip cookies. Enough for the whole class," Mrs. Sweet said. "I figured all that Gifted and Talented thinking might make you hungry."

Adam knew she shouldn't be there. But

the smell of her freshly baked cookies *was* making everyone hungry.

"I guess it's okay this time," Adam said. He reached for the plate of cookies, but Mrs. Sweet jerked it away.

"I'll hand them out, dearie," she said. "You just go on with what you were doing."

Mrs. Sweet barged into the classroom

and started handing out the cookies.

Adam could see that J didn't know what to do. He still had things he needed to tell the class. But Mrs. Sweet wasn't cleared by IM-8 to hear what he had to say.

"Don't mind me, dearie," Mrs. Sweet said to J. "You go right ahead and talk."

"Show us the pencil with rockets on it!" one of the new agents said. Adam glanced down at a seating chart. The new agent was Pierre Latour from Paris, France. *Could he be the one?* Adam wondered.

"A pencil with rockets!" Mrs. Sweet exclaimed. "Oh, my goodness! What in the world is that, dearie?"

Now the sweat was pouring off J's face. This was a big-time security breakdown. Adam held his breath.

"Just a pencil Gifted and Talented kids can use to take their tests," J said. "We also have one with kitty-cats on it."

Adam let out his breath. J had been nice *and* hadn't given away any secrets. He was a real pro.

Mrs. Sweet hung around for a few more minutes. "Well, I don't understand any of this stuff, dearie," she said, "so I'd better go bake some more chocolate chip cookies."

Adam felt bad for her. She must be lonely.

The bell rang. The IM-8 agents went to their next classes. "I have secret disguises now," Magna told Adam.

"Me too," groaned Kay. "I'm lousy at disguises. It's my worst subject."

Kay and Magna left together. Tulip and Adam stayed behind to clean up Mrs. Sweet's cookies.

They had each just eaten their third one when Tulip gasped. *"Ja!* Magna was right! These chocolate chips really *are* in patterns!"

Adam looked at the cookie he was holding. His chocolate chips were in the shape of a triangle.

Oh, no! Adam thought. *It can't be true!* There was a chocolate chip code baked into Mrs. Sweet's cookies!

4

The

Chocolate Chip Code

"Z's code-breaking class is about to start, Tulip," Adam said. "Come on! We have to crack this code!"

Adam quickly tapped out an urgent message on his watch. It went straight to Magna's belt buckle receiver. In minutes, Kay and Magna had asked for bathroom passes and met Adam and Tulip.

"We're in big trouble!" Adam told them.
"I hope Z can help us."

Z showed the class all kinds of codes—
math codes, alphabet codes, and secret
writing codes.

But none of those were what Adam

needed. He raised his hand. "What about chocolate chips?" he asked.

Some of the newer spies giggled.

They'll never make it as IM-8 agents! Adam thought scornfully.

"In China, there is a chocolate chip code," Z said. "But very few people know it."

"Blimey!" Magna whispered. "I knew something was suspicious about those cookies!"

"Dude! Maybe Mrs. Sweet isn't so sweet," Kay said.

"*Ja!* It makes sense, Adam," Tulip said.

Adam knew they were telling the truth. "This is my fault," he admitted. "I wanted

Mrs. Sweet to cook for Spy School."

Adam decided not to tell them that he'd also thought she'd make a good IM-8 agent!

After class, Adam went up to Z. "Someone here at Spy School knows the chocolate chip code," he said. "We need to know it, too."

Z wrote the code on the chalkboard.

Adam and the girls studied it carefully.

"Brilliant!" Magna said.

Adam slammed his palm against his forehead. "Now I know how IM-8 secrets are getting out!"

"How?" Kay asked.

"Mrs. Sweet gives them to the driver of the big black car," Adam said. "Those chocolate chip cookies are not going to the nursing home! They're going to our enemies!"

"Blimey!" Magna said. "We have to stop this!"

"I have a plan," Adam said grimly. "Meet me by the cafeteria at midnight."

5

The Cookie Switch

Adam couldn't sleep. He had been betrayed by Mrs. Sweet! Did this mean his career in IM-8 was over?

At five minutes before midnight, he got off his cot, put on his tuxedo, and slipped out of the gym. Tulip, Magna, and Kay met him outside the door to the cafeteria. "Do we have Mrs. Sweet's cookie recipe?" Tulip asked.

"We're in luck," Adam said. He held up an empty chocolate chip bag. "She uses the recipe on the back."

They sneaked into the cafeteria.

This was one of Adam's most difficult missions. He had to bake cookies in a dark kitchen while an evil spy who looked like a kindly grandmother slept on a cot nearby.

Slowly, quietly, they mixed together all the ingredients except the chocolate chips.

Just as the dough was almost ready, Mrs. Sweet turned over on her cot. "One row of five chips!" she shouted. "One row of three!" Then she let out a loud snore.

Adam and the girls dived under the

table. "Mrs. Sweet is calling out the chocolate chip code in her sleep!" Adam whispered.

Mrs. Sweet made no further sounds. They crawled out from under the table.

"What phony information are we going to put in the cookies?" Kay asked.

Adam was prepared. "IM-8 is moving its headquarters to the top of a volcano in Hawaii!" he said. He looked at Magna. "Can you make the chocolate chips say that?"

"Right-o!" Magna said.

She grabbed a handful of chocolate chips and started pressing them into the cookie dough.

When she finished, she said, "There! Now we bake them at 375 degrees for ten minutes or until they're golden brown."

Ten minutes later, the cookies were done. After they had cooled, Adam replaced the ones Mrs. Sweet had baked with the ones they had baked.

They sneaked out of the cafeteria.

"Dude! We have one problem," Kay said. "What do we do with Mrs. Sweet's cookies?"

They took the cookies to an empty classroom. Magna decoded them.

"If that information had gotten out, IM-8 would have been finished!" Kay said.

"We were lucky this time," Adam said.

They decided to eat all the cookies so that none of IM-8's secrets would fall into the wrong hands.

The next morning at breakfast, they all sat together.

Mrs. Sweet was carefully watching the clock on the cafeteria wall.

"It won't be long now," Adam said.

Mrs. Sweet picked up the box of cookies and headed out a side door.

Adam and the girls quickly followed. They hid behind a bush just as the big black car pulled up in front of the school.

Through the branches, Adam saw Mrs. Sweet hand the box of cookies to the driver.

The driver opened the box, studied the cookies closely, and said, "Heh! Heh! Heh! Our work here is finished! Heh! Heh! Heh!"

Mrs. Sweet gave the driver a puzzled look. "It is?" she said.

"Yes, my dear wife! Heh! Heh! Heh!" the driver said. "Let's take a little vacation to Hawaii!"

The driver pulled Mrs. Sweet into the big black car, and it roared away from the school.

Adam gasped. "That was my archenemy, General Menace! I should have known he was the one behind this!"

"That means Mrs. Sweet is really Mrs. Menace!" the girls cried.

They ran and told T everything that had happened.

"Good work! That buys us some time," T said. "We'll beef up IM-8 security to make sure this never happens again."

"We need to hurry, sir," Tulip said.

"Mrs. Sweet is smart," Magna said. "It won't take her long to figure out that IM-8 isn't moving its headquarters to Hawaii!"

"That's true," Adam said. "And while you're at it, you also need to make the IM-8 obstacle course harder."

Tulip, Magna, and Kay looked at him. "Why?" they asked.

"Well, if *General Menace* can pass the test . . ."

"General Menace?" Tulip cried.

Adam nodded. "That was General Menace spying on us."

"Are you sure?" T said.

"I'm positive. He couldn't pass up the chance to watch IM-8 agents at work," Adam explained. "It all makes sense."

"Then that's your first job, Sharp!" T said. "A brand-new obstacle course!"

"You'll need to give the project to someone else, sir," Adam said. He handed

T a letter. "I'm resigning from IM-8."

The girls gasped.

"Why?" T demanded.

"It's simple, sir," Adam said. "I'm the one who wanted Mrs. Sweet—uh, Mrs. *Menace*—to cook for Spy School."

"And *that* was a brilliant idea, Sharp," T said. "It was the only way to find out how General Menace and his wife sent secret messages to their spies around the world! Now they'll never be able to use the chocolate chip code again!"

Adam thought for a minute. "I guess you're right, sir," he said. "It really was clever!" He took the letter back from T and tore it up.

"Dude!" Kay said. "IM-8 wouldn't be the same without you!"

"*Ja!*" Tulip said. "You're the best!"

"Blimey, Adam! You shouldn't scare us like that!" Magna said.

Adam grinned. He was back for good. And General Menace had better watch out!